For
Betty Gowan
with my love
Mildred Cram

To for
Betty Gowan

THE PROMISE

THE PROMISE

BY

MILDRED CRAM

❧ *1949* ☙

ALFRED A. KNOPF·NEW YORK

❀⟩❀⟩ *TO MOTHER*

✧✦✧✦✧✦✧✦✧✦✧✦✧

THE PROMISE

✧✦✧✦✧✦✧✦✧✦✧✦✧

THEY stopped at the Last Chance service station for gas and an oil check. It was raining, just enough to spangle the windshield, and the night air was moist and warm.

Alicia had been driving while Pat dozed. Now she rolled the window down and smiled at the attendant.

"Ten gallons, please."

The boy glanced up, and Pat caught the look he gave Alicia . . . there was a whistle in it.

"I'm driving from here on in," Pat said abruptly.

He got out and, borrowing the attendant's chamois, wiped off the windows and the headlights. He didn't want the boy to look at Alicia again.

When he opened the car door on the driver's side, she had moved over and was peering into the mirror of her compact, blending the color on her lips with the tip of her little finger. She had taken off her hat and had tossed it into the back seat, where it lay upside down on top of her suitcase. Her red hair, smooth and burnished, was cut short like that of Joan of Arc . . . she had the Maid's direct, clean beauty.

2

Pat slid under the wheel and drove away from the station into the dark. He heard the click of the compact, then saw Alicia's fingers groping for the lighter.

"Smoke?" he asked.

"Please."

"In my pocket. And light one for me, will you?"

Presently her hand came around and she put the cigarette between his lips. He thought with sudden bitterness how often she had made this gesture during the days of their happiness, the way a woman does a small service for her beloved, gently, her shoulder touching his. . . . Tonight she simply gave him a lighted cigarette.

As if she had heard his thoughts, Alicia said: "The thrill's gone, isn't it, Pat? I remember when just to be with you like this, driving somewhere—anywhere—was enough. . . ."

Pat interrupted sharply: "Let's not talk about it until we get home. You're tired and I'm sore. No matter what we say, we'll hurt each other."

"All right," she said. "But it's over, and we both know it."

It was raining now in earnest; big drops like pellets bounced and glistened in the headlights. The road began to lift, between whitewashed railings. Beyond, and below, the darkest dark of a canyon, the massed black of trees, down and down. . . .

"Please don't drive too fast," Alicia said. "I'd like to get there in one piece, if you don't mind."

"Okay."

Pat opened the window and leaned out to watch the white line. They were almost at the crest, three or four thousand feet above the valley. He reckoned that, be the good Lord willing, he could make San Francisco before dawn. Here in the mountains there was little or no traffic, and, once down the grade, he'd drive at any speed he liked. He wanted above everything to get home.

3

The whole trip had been a mistake.

Alicia had to make a personal appearance at the opening of a new radio station. Following her Friday broadcast, they drove to Salt Lake City. Pat realized now that he should have let her fly, alone. But for a long time they had been making desperately formal gestures, like a pair of polite enemies, and Pat had convinced himself that what they needed was a chance to talk to each other.

He had guessed wrong.

For the first time in their married life they had had nothing to say.

And here they were, hurrying back, their love still unraveling, like an old sweater sleeve when a thread breaks.

Leaning forward, Alicia switched on the radio. A dance band sifted through a sharp crackle of static. She dialed past into a bedlam of overlapping stations. She was fishing, Pat knew, for San

Francisco. . . . Suddenly the announcer's familiar voice faded in: "Listen tomorrow, and every day, Monday through Friday, to Alicia Adams. . . ."

Pat could feel her smiling beside him in the dark as she tuned out again.

They had reached the top of the pass and he drew off the road and parked. The pounding weight of water on the convertible's canvas top was so loud that for a moment they seemed to be contained within a roar of drums. Then, abruptly, the rain stopped. And Pat asked the question he had been shying away from for six months:

"Is there someone else, Alicia?"

"No," she said. "There never could be."

"What is it you want, then?"

After a moment she said:

"Success. I'm sold on success, Pat! I want to be Somebody with a capital S. A radio personality as important as Jo Stafford or Peggy Lee. Tops."

"You think you can climb faster alone. Is that it?"

"Yes."

Pat snapped on the ignition and kicked at the starter.

"All right. You can divorce me if you like. I won't stand in your way!"

He jerked the car into the road. The headlights swung and probed at the descent. Far down the grade, a Greyhound circled the buttresses, climbed toward the crest. And presently with a shriek of giant tires, a displacement that Pat felt in his ears, it passed. In the mirror he saw the red taillight blink and vanish. Oddly enough, he was reminded that Christmas was only a week away, and a strange, ugly self-pity made him say: "You might have waited until after Christmas!"

"Let's leave the holly and mistletoe out of it, shall we?"

"Sure. Let's be realistic. Let's be modern and kick sentiment in the teeth!"

"It's easier," Alicia said. "And, if you ask me, a lot more civilized."

4

To steady himself, Pat watched the road. The whitewashed guard-posts seemed to turn in slow circles, like dancers. On this side of the pass, curtains of misty rain, fine as gauze, swept across the road. Ahead, curving across a deep canyon, he saw the Snow Creek bridge. He had crossed it many times, always with caution, because the highway approaches were too narrow, badly graded, dangerous. A car was entering the span at the other end, a quarter of a mile away, and, as a precaution, Pat slowed down and kept well over to the right.

He was thinking with furious bitterness that he would have preferred a physical battle—hair-pulling and slapping—to this freezingly amiable discussion. He and Alicia had given joy and beauty to each other. Whose fault was it that they had become strangers?

"Pat!" she screamed suddenly. "Isn't that car on the wrong side?"

It was, and coming fast.

"Pat!"

With a flash of sick fear through his heart, Pat used the brakes. The approaching car hurtled straight at them, and for a second the windshield was blind with glare.

"Look out!"

Pat's flesh recoiled before the blow; he ducked his head. The onrushing car tore along the con-vertible's side and sped on.

"The fence!" Alicia screamed.

9 ✦✧✦✧

They slipped slowly, helplessly, toward the railing. The wheel spun in Pat's hands. There were no brakes. The white barrier splintered and they went through, dropping steeply down a slope of muddy earth. . . .

"Pat! Pat!"

Down, with ponderous deliberation. . . . The heavy car twisted, slithered, sank deeper and deeper, lurched, and stopped.

"That's it," Pat said. "Get out, quick!"

Alicia sat where she was, laughing the shrill laughter of hysterical fear.

"Shut up!" Pat shouted.

Her laughter stopped on a caught breath. She slid under the wheel and jumped down beside him.

"I'm sorry," he said awkwardly. "I can't tell how far the bank goes—there may be a long drop into the river. . . . Here, give me your hand."

They struggled up to the splintered railing and, on the bridge again, took stock of themselves. No broken bones; just a lot of sticky mud, like plaster of Paris. . . . But shock ran cold in their veins. Their teeth chattered. Their hands shook.

"God," Pat said under his breath. "That was a close one."

He peered down into the dark. "Another ten

feet and it would have been curtains for both of us. . . ."

Far below, the sound of rushing water—a cold, clear, swift sound—gave him the measure of the depth they had escaped. The rain played a delicate accompaniment to that more dominant theme, and there was a rustle and whisper of trees. Wilderness music, beautiful and lonely. . . .

5

"Here comes a car," Pat said as cheerfully as he could. He stepped into the blurred beam of the oncoming headlights and waved his arms. But the car sped past, ignoring his frantic signal.

Alicia huddled in her coat; her hair was drenched; she wept with misery.

"Oh, why did *this* have to happen? I mustn't catch cold! I *mustn't!*"

Pat said he'd try to get a blanket out of the car, and, climbing through the fence again, started down.

The convertible had turned completely around and now hung with its rear wheels over the brink. Pat felt, rather than saw, its final plunge. He waited a split second for the crash. Metal on rock. A crunching impact. . . .

As he stood, ankle-deep in mud, staring into the void, a gust of wind in the canyon below parted the massed branches of the trees, revealing a light. It flickered off and on like a star. . . .

Pat waded back to the bridge and told Alicia: "I think there's a house in the canyon. . . . I'll go down and see. Wait here."

But Alicia followed him. Beneath the immense concrete pier that supported the first span, a rough path, used during construction, descended to the creek.

"Give me your hand." Pat said again.

Pausing now and then to strike a match, he led the way down between heaps of shag and broken rock. Presently the great bridge was above them and the sound of rushing water was loud and wonderful, like a challenging voice. They followed the stream into the forest and again Pat saw the light. As they hurried toward it, there was a crackling in the brush, the thud of small hoofs.

"Deer," Pat said.

A few hundred yards beyond, they came to a clearing. And a house.

6

Pat's first thought was that he had imagined it, had evoked it for some purpose of his own. Built of field stone, deeply embrasured, it stood behind a fence made of uneven, whitewashed sticks laced with rope. The tin roof glistened like the silvery scales of a fish. Smoke rose from a stone chimney, a blue gauze pillar, straight up into the rain. The light Pat had seen from the bridge fanned out from a small window set high in the wall. . . .

He unlatched the gate. He had learned caution at strange doors, but before he could knock, this one opened. A man stood on the threshold. Beside him two bushy-haired dogs bristled and growled.

The man was tall, thin, white-haired. He carried an oil lamp, which he held above his head so that Pat was able, at once, to see his face—a face stern, gentle, and sorrowful. He wore a clean blue shirt and a sleeveless sweater.

"My name's Adams," Pat began. "This is my wife, Alicia. A hit-run driver knocked us off the bridge. . . ."

"I know," the old man interrupted. "I heard the crash. I expected you."

He stood aside.

13 ✧✧✧

"Come in," he said. "You are welcome."

Pat and Alicia followed him into the house.

7

The room they entered was long and narrow; the pitched roof gave it a magical proportion. The walls were of stone, three feet thick, and whitewashed. A wide hearth, blackened by the smoke of countless fires, faced the door. A log burned there now, and the room was sweet with the scent of pine cones. Boiling sap bubbled in the flames.

Putting the lamp down, the old man opened a wall cupboard and reached inside for a dented and lopsided coffeepot.

"You musn't go to any trouble," Alicia said. "If we can just sit here until morning. . . ."

"I always make coffee for them," the old man interrupted. "It's very comforting."

He filled the coffeepot with water ladled from a stone crock and, crossing to the hearth, raked the hot ashes forward to make a small cone. In this miniature crater he placed the pot. Then, straightening, he said:

"Take off your coats. Hang them here to dry. . . ."

He indicated a chair, broad, sturdy, intricately carved, which faced the hearth.

Pat removed his jacket. It was a favorite of his, tailored in London when he was on leave there in '44.

To his amazement, the sleeves were slashed from shoulder to wrist, and there was a jagged rent over the heart. . . . Alicia's skirt, too, was ripped; her stockings were in ribbons; her coat was torn across the back between the shoulders.

Pat stared.

"I don't understand," he began. "We're not scratched, either of us. . . ."

"They never understand, at first," the old man interrupted. He shook his head. "They go on thinking they're alive. . . . I try to tell them— but they won't believe me. . . ."

"Well, *we're* alive, all right!" Pat laughed. "You can see for yourself!"

The old man looked from Pat to Alicia. He glanced at the torn and slashed coats. But he said nothing. The coffee boiled up, creamed over, and sizzled into the hot ashes. He lifted the pot with a forked stick and set it aside on the hearth.

"I'll get some goat's milk for you," he said. "I keep it fresh and cold in the creek. . . . Wait here by the fire."

The dogs followed him, and as the door closed, Alicia whispered: "Pat! He thinks we're dead!"

"I know. He's a little touched, I guess."

"Just for a minute, I couldn't help thinking we might be—"

"Nonsense."

"Well—if we *were*—it would be sort of wonderful, wouldn't it? No pain, or blood, or anything. . . . And being here—"

She looked around the room.

"When I was a kid, I had a story-book. There was a picture in it I've never forgotten. A room like this. . . ."

Suddenly she held out her arm.

"Pinch me! See if I feel it!"

Pat shook his head.

"No, you don't! We're strangers. Remember?"

He turned away and, to avoid her eyes, prowled around the room. "I'll bet the old man built this place himself, stone by stone," he said. "How solid it is—rooted deep—like a tree! Why can't all houses feel like this? Most of them float on the surface, like rafts. . . ."

He paused, staring up at a shelf crowded with small figures carved out of some sort of smooth, dark wood.

"Look at these. They must be his. . . ."

Alicia came to stand beside him.

"Wonderful, aren't they?"

"And see here—a cuckoo clock! A real one!"

Pat glanced at his wrist.

"I wonder if it works. We'll know in three seconds!"

The heavy pendulum ticked-tocked with a sort of purposeful deliberation, as if it was in no hurry . . . no hurry . . . no hurry. . . .

Suddenly, on the second of ten o'clock, a hoarse whirring and grinding began within the casing, a labored breathing in preparation for great accomplishment. The door in the fretted tower flew open with a bang, a bird jumped out, said *Cuckoo* ten times, and jumped back again. The door slammed. The clock sighed, the whirring stopped, and once more the pendulum ticked and tocked . . . no hurry . . . no hurry. . . .

"This place stirs up my imagination like a long spoon in a drink!" Pat said.

"I'm surprised." Alicia smiled, with sweet mockery. "I thought you preferred the 'uncompromising simplicity' of the modern! Or do I quote you correctly?"

Pat saw the trap he had set for himself. "I like beauty," he insisted, "wherever I find it. I could work here. That book of mine would write itself."

He turned to Alicia with a sudden flash of hope, a profound urgency.

"Suppose I could talk the old man into renting the place? Not for long. A year, maybe. I've got a thousand in the bank. We could toss our jobs over the moon and really live, up here. Would you do it? Would you be happy?"

"I'd be bored to death," she cried. "You know I would! Why do you ask? To make me seem selfish?"

Before Pat could answer, the old man opened the door. He had brought milk and a crock of cheese from the creek.

8

He drew a table into the circle of firelight and sat down with Pat and Alicia. The dogs lay beside him and two cats that had been asleep on a shelf jumped down to crouch over a bowl of goat's milk.

Pat wasn't hungry. He felt strangely drowsy, as if under an enchantment. He realized now how long it had been since he had heard any silence other than the empty silence of the city in the hours before dawn. The night here was full of the rumors of rain and wind and moving trees and the busy voice of Snow Creek, running free over the cold stones. . . .

The old man broke thick chunks of corn bread and crumbled them together with the cold bacon.

"The beaver-trappers taught me this," he explained. "Many years ago, when I first came to America."

"You weren't born in this country, then?"

"No. I am Swiss. I was born near Thun, seventy-five years ago. My name is Peter Fauner."

He explained that the death of his young wife had driven him away from his home. Seeking forgetfulness, he had wandered across the world, working when he could, at all sorts of jobs. He had been a miner, a farmer, a lumberman, a sailor. When at last he discovered Snow Creek, he stayed, because it reminded him of the forests and cold streams of his canton. He found that goats could live in the flowery pastures above his house, and soon the wild animals learned to trust him. But they were scarce, and growing scarcer. Cars and busses were bringing hunters into the wilderness —at certain seasons, the crack of rifles echoed against the canyon walls day and night. . . .

During the construction of the bridge, he said, the wild creatures retreated from the sound of blasting and hammering. But not for long. The day came when the workmen departed. The lofty span was dedicated, and traffic stayed up there where it belonged.

Peter Fauner, in his stone house, could see the endless flow of cars, and when the wind was right he could hear the swish and rumble of their passage, the clash of gears on the pass, and sometimes—too often—the shock of collision. . . .

9

Twenty people had lost their lives on the Snow Creek bridge.

A farmer and his wife—middle-aged Kansans— were the first.

"They came to my door," Peter Fauner explained, "just as you did tonight. I had watched the ambulance take the bodies away, and so I was shocked when I saw them. I thought what you're thinking: that I was out of my mind. But I took them in. They were frightened, helpless, like lost children. . . ."

"How long did they stay with you?" Alicia asked politely.

"A few hours. . . . In the morning I asked them what they wanted to do. They said they hoped to go to heaven."

The old man smiled.

"Now, I asked myself, where is heaven? I'd never given much thought to such things. But I supposed it was up—in the sky. And so I cut some staffs and carved their names on them—Beth and Joel Burnet. I remember very well. And the date—March the 10th, in 1920."

Peter met Pat's skeptical eyes. His look was direct and steady.

"Then," he said, "I led them as far as I could, to the summit of the mountain called Whiteface, six thousand feet. They thanked me and said good-by to me there. And went on."

There was a pause, filled only with the un-hurried ticking of the clock.

"I stood in the snow for a long time watching them. . . . They seemed to climb a trail of light —up and up—until at last they disappeared."

"I hope they made it all right," Pat said.

"They always do."

"Were there others, then?"

"Many. Men. Women. Children—"

Peter broke off.

"The children," he said after a moment, "were afraid. Until they saw—"

Again, he hesitated.

"Someone always came down the trail to meet the children," he said finally.

10

Pat thought: "Crazy, of course! Nice old guy. But off the beam."

Yet Peter Fauner had the look of a practical man. His face, now that Pat could watch and study it, expressed, not confusion, but a calm ac-ceptance, as if he had conquered something re-bellious within himself. It was not a saintly face, nor was it benign. Rather, hard experience and loneliness had carved deeply into it. His hair was ash-white, dull, thick, and upstanding. Only his eyes were defiantly young, eager, yet shy . . . they looked away from Pat's scrutiny.

When they had finished eating, he began to clear the table, but Alicia jumped up. "Let me," she said. "Where's the dishpan? And the soap?"

She looked very lovely with the sleeves of her torn blouse rolled up. Carefully she washed and stacked the dishes.

Pat decided to go with the old man when he took the milk and cheese crocks back to the creek.

The path led through a thicket, past a cave where the goats were tethered behind wire. Peter Fauner called to them and there was a tinkle of bells, a flat nanny-blatting in the dark.

Pat could hear the creek, but he couldn't see it. Peter stopped and knelt, placing the stone crocks in shallow water. The smell of melted snow was in the air, acrid, icy. Pat was again aware of animals near by . . . the same crackle and pad and parting of the thicket he had heard in the clearing.

"My creatures," Peter Fauner explained. "They are coming close for the winter. When it snows, I feed them. And they never forget. Nor do I."

Alicia was putting the dishes back in the cupboard, hanging the cups on their proper hooks. When Pat and the old man came in, she said:

"I'm sleepy. Could we go to bed, please?"

Peter Fauner explained that he had no beds. Instead he brought some heavy quilts and spread them on the floor near the hearth. He himself, he said, always sat in the carved chair at night. He slept very little.

"When you are old, you treasure consciousness. I like to watch the fire and listen to little sounds. . . ."

He smiled.

"But you two must rest tonight. Tomorrow you have a long way to go."

Alicia stretched out, with Pat beside her, yet apart from her. He lay with his hands clasped behind his head. He was aware of the fast beating of his heart, an unpleasant sense of excitement, of tension.

In a corner of the room, stacked against the wall, there were perhaps a dozen tall sticks; freshly cut, the outshoots had been peeled away, leaving green scars. Peter ran his finger along the smooth bark, testing first one, then another. He selected two. Then, blowing out the lamp, he sat in the fire-light, the sharp blade of a small knife cutting and slicing, so that wafers of wood drifted to powder the fur of the dogs asleep at his feet.

Pat watched.

The name "Alicia" took shape on the staff.

And for a moment he let himself believe that to-morrow he would climb with her to paradise. . . .

Better far, he thought, than failure here on earth . . . ugliness . . . divorce. . . .

Suddenly Peter Fauner spoke: "Why don't you take her in your arms?" he asked. "She is your wife. You died today, together. Why do you lie apart now?"

Pat turned to Alicia.

"Why do we?"

With a strange smile she looked at Pat intently, then turned and entered the familiar embrace. He flung his arm across her, heavily, but he didn't kiss her, although that was perhaps what she wanted.

She reached up and touched his hair. She was like that. Any other woman would have spoken, and in speaking would have broken the spell. Alicia's fingers did the talking: "Let it be like this, if it's only for tonight."

Peter glanced down at them with an unreadable expression, then returned to his carving. After a while Pat forgot that the old man was there. He watched Alicia, thinking back to the beginning . . . their meeting. . . .

12

He had been with the 47th Tank Battalion in France.

After the hell of Hatten, Able Company and the Medics rested at Friedolsheim.

Alicia came with the first USO show. She was twenty then. With a warm, husky voice, a voice that had love in it, something compassionate and deeply feminine. . . .

Pat was one of the lucky few who managed to meet her. They couldn't be alone, but they could look at each other. Their eyes took inventory. She promised to write, and her letters caught up with him all the way to Mühldorf. For her, the hope of getting back to her, he fought. And survived.

When word came that the war was over, his first thought was for her. Then the other, unbearable thoughts took over, and he was ashamed to be happy, ashamed to be alive, because of those left along the bloody road . . . good men like Tharpe . . . all the others. . . .

Alicia was waiting for him in New York. And the day they were married she made an awkward little speech: "I don't like to promise it'll be forever, darling," she said. "But I've got my fingers crossed! Maybe we'll be lucky!"

For their honeymoon they pooled their savings and drove across the continent in a second-hand jeep. Pat looked at his country with both love and foreboding; it was like watching a noble church in the path of a division. Pat sensed that his service was not over. He had climbed out of his tank for the last time, but he still had fighting to do.

At first it was Pat's future, Pat's success, that mattered.

Since his mother and father lived in San Francisco, he took Alicia there to live. They packed away their uniforms and ribbons and set up housekeeping in a three-room flat on Signal Hill. From the windows they could see the Ferry Tower and the bridge and the arrival and departure of ships. . . .

And Pat looked for, and found, a job in radio.

Journeyman stuff, but a chance to master the technique. One year. Two years. . . . Somehow he couldn't get to serious writing. He was a radio hack, and the things he needed to say backed up in him and hurt so that he couldn't sleep. . . .

Then it was Alicia's turn.

One day she impressed a record with the love in her voice. The disk spun. The mike picked it up. It went out over the air-waves, into houses, into human hearts—that rich husky, caressing voice that Pat had tried to capture and to hold for himself. . . .

Alicia was on her way. . . .

"Listen, every day, Monday through Friday."

13

"Pat," she asked suddenly, "will the car ever run again, do you suppose?"

"We'll see, tomorrow. But I doubt it."

"How long is it to morning?"

"An hour or two."

With the tip of her finger she traced the line of his profile from forehead to chin.

"You look nice in the firelight," she said.

"So do you."

She whispered: "We're lovely ghosts, aren't we?"

"Alicia—" he began.

"Don't say it, Pat!"

"I've been thinking about us—the beginning. It would be swell, wouldn't it, to feel like that again?"

"We never will, Pat."

"Why not? Why couldn't we?"

"Because we want different things! I want the Big Time. And you want to write a great book. Pretty soon, if we have to sacrifice for each other, we'll be enemies."

"I suppose so."

His arm tightened around her.

"Listen, Alicia. I *want* you to succeed. Only not now. Not quite yet. Don't you see? First I've got to justify my own existence—"

He broke off, hurt and baffled. She had fallen asleep.

"Alicia! You weren't listening!"

She opened her eyes.

"I'm awfully tired, Pat. Let's not go over and over it. . . ."

"Okay. Go back to sleep."

"Kiss me first."

Her lips were warm and sweet, warmer and sweeter than they had been for a long time. Presently she unbuttoned his collar, slipped her hand inside his shirt, and fell asleep that way.

Pat thought: "She has shared the best in my life so far." He thought of all the hilarious things they had done together. How the most sober happenings inevitably turned into a laugh for them.

They had never had a date that wasn't charged with excitement, because they had remained lovers. . . . And that was good.

But Pat had believed that there was better to come with the passing years. Home. A center of experience and growth. Children. . . . The unfolding. The experiment. . . . Finally, with old age, their rich harvest. . . .

He glanced up at Peter Fauner. The woodcarver's expression was grave and gentle.

"You love her," he said simply.

"Sure I do."

"Why aren't you happy, then?"

"Me?" Pat asked, surprised.

"Both of you."

14

Pat sat up. Without waking, Alicia turned on her side and folded both hands under her cheek.

"Things around us have separated us, I guess," Pat said slowly. He groped for a cigarette. "We're both restless. Pushing our luck. . . . Alicia's a radio singer. All she thinks of is her job. She won't be happy until she's on top. And then she won't be happy! She'll be wise as hell, that's all."

"And you?"

"Oh, I'm the switched-off poet of the airways! Meeting a deadline, too, every day. Neither of us has time for the growth of love."

Peter Fauner set Alicia's staff aside.

"There will be all the time in the world," he said, "where you are going now."

"You seem very sure that we died up there on the bridge!"

Without answering, Peter lifted and examined the other staff. Turning it between his palms, testing it for weight and strength.

Pat's scalp prickled when he saw his own name taking shape under the blade.

He cried suddenly: "I wish you wouldn't do that!"

"It's no trouble at all."

Peter Fauner paused and listened to a new silence.

"Do you hear? The rain has stopped. The wind —it comes now from the north. Tomorrow will be fair. Then in a few days it will snow."

He shook his head, frowning.

"Snow," he repeated. "My poor creatures. . . ."

15

Pat was a little ashamed of his outburst. He listened to the rustle of ashes in the embers on the hearth. The deliberate clock. The scampering of some small animal across the roof.

He hadn't wanted to think of the war tonight. Not here in this room. Not tonight. . . .

But suddenly he remembered. . . . He tried to turn his mind away, to look aside. As always, when the terrible vision of Hatten assailed him, he was forced to see the village again—the dead in the street, the girl who ran screaming out from a cellar, the roofless houses, the blasted walls. It was as if he were inside a lurching tank, his foot on the firing-trigger, his eyes glued to the telescopic sight, moving inexorably upon chaos.

With a groan he sat up, his hands over his eyes.

"What is it?" Peter asked.

"War. I think about it sometimes. I hate its gaudy guts!"

After a silence Peter said:

"War is over for you."

Pat shook his head.

"No, it's *not* over for me! I've still got to write about it—put in my dime's worth for the guys who don't know what it's like!"

He got to his feet and went to the hearth.

"Adventure? Escape? I'll make 'em look at the bloody truth of it!"

Embarrassed, he grinned and kicked at the logs, sending up a shower of sparks.

"You can throw that staff away! I won't need it!"

But the name "Patrick" continued to take shape. The firelight reflected on the knife-blade in the woodcarver's hand made it look like a darting flame. Pat watched, hypnotized, until, exhausted,

he stretched out again beside Alicia and fell
asleep. *

16

When he woke, the room was cold and the windows were faint squares of gray.

He had learned to come instantly from sleep
into full consciousness.

The door was open. Old Peter Fauner stood on
the threshold, looking out into the yard. Pat went
to stand beside him. Rumpling his hair and
stretching, he said cheerfully: "Good morning!"

"Good morning! We have a fine day!"

The air was clean, sweet with the scent of
washed resin and fern. Beyond the fence some deer
grazed on a narrow strip of alfalfa; their jaws
chopped and cut. Pat could see their antlers—half-
moons in the faint light.

Closer to the house, rabbits and small red foxes
ate together from tin bowls. And, as Pat watched, a
small bear padded up the steps and pressed his
cold, wet muzzle into the palm of his hand. The

contact was so unfamiliar as to be exquisite, yet it startled him and he laughed uneasily.

"That's never happened to me before," he said.

"You are spirit now," Peter stated calmly.

He put his hand in the bear's pelt and half-led, half-pushed the little animal through the gate and toward the creek.

Pat turned back into the house. Suddenly, with desperate urgency, he wanted to escape. . . . The sensation was akin to mortal fear; as if he stood on the brink of the grave.

He woke Alicia, pulled her to her feet. She leaned against him, crumpled and blurred with sleep. . . .

"It's dark. What time is it?"

"Listen, Alicia. The old man's down at the creek. Let's get out of here!"

"But Pat—"

"Don't stop to argue! Here's your coat. Quick! Put it on!"

"No, Pat. *No.* . . . We can't. He's so sure we were sent to him! If we run away, we'll be letting him down!"

Pat hesitated, one arm in the tattered sleeve of

his jacket. She was right, of course, and he loved her for it. He was puzzled, too.

"How about your show this afternoon?"

"I'll get there," she said, "if I'm supposed to! But right now let's play along with Peter—at least, until we think of something. . . ."

Pat put his hands on her shoulders and made her look at him.

"You poor kid! You believe we're dead, don't you?"

She shook her head. "I don't know *what* I believe, Pat. We *might* be! And if we *are*—"

She caught her breath.

"He seems to know the way, doesn't he?"

Pat held her close, patting her back.

"Both of us. We're scared stiff, and no wonder! That was a bad smash . . . and our clothes and everything. . . ."

He shook Alicia gently.

"Let me take care of this."

"What can you tell him?"

"That he's mistaken. And thanks, but we've got to get back to our jobs."

Hearing Peter Fauner at the door, Pat broke off.

Peter seemed to enter with the sun.

A shaft of gold made a path across the room, and the tall, straight old man walked in light. He had brought fresh goat's milk, and again he brewed strong coffee and crumbled bread for them.

It occurred to Pat that Peter would refuse payment for his hospitality. And so he asked, as casually as he could, whether the woodcarvings were for sale.

The old man's eyes twinkled.

"I know why you offer to buy my work," he said, "but they are not for sale—to you."

Alicia pointed to the head of a girl—a laughing girl with a tilted nose, her braided hair crowned with a circlet of flowers.

"Not even this one?" she asked. "She's so very lovely. . . ."

Peter held the small image in the palm of his hand. It might have been a butterfly pulsing and fluttering there.

"Once," he said, "she belonged to me—the girl herself. She was my wife."

He put the carving down and turned away.

"It's time to go," he said gruffly.

Pat thought: "Now! Tell him!"

But he found himself accepting the staff Peter held out to him with a polite murmur of thanks!

18

Outside, the world was decked with jewels. Raindrops glittered on every pine needle, every leaf. Liquid emeralds, sapphires, and diamonds shook and blazed in the sun. Sudden flashes of topaz seemed to explode in midair and to be replaced by rubies. The sky was taller and deeper than any sky Pat had ever seen.

He struck the staff lightly against the earth, thinking that so must pilgrims feel—dedicated and full of dignity.

Peter Fauner paused at the cave to release the goats, then turned aside from Snow Creek and followed a steep path up through the forest.

He carried no staff, and walked slowly, but with co-ordinated grace, in his scuffed, worn shoes, the dogs making contact with his heels.

Once Pat turned and looked down at the bridge.

He could see the car, a crumpled ruin, and the crimson eye of a cop's parked cycle.

Yet he was drawn inevitably on, and up. Alicia followed, close behind, singing as she climbed. . . . Answering birds flashed in the treetops. And an echo, tossed back from a far canyon wall, filled the air with singing Alicias.

An hour had passed when the heavy stand of pine trees thinned, giving way to a rocky pasture. Beyond, a granite slope surged against the strong buttresses of the range. And still higher, Whiteface, crested with snow, broke like a wave upon the dark blue of the sky.

Peter halted.

"There," he said, pointing, "the mountain! If you climb the west flank, you'll have no trouble. . . . You should reach the summit before nightfall."

"You're coming with us, of course?"

Peter shook his head.

"No."

Again he gave them that searching look.

"I am an old man. My Swiss heart, geared to such effort, is rusty and tired. . . ."

He held out his hand.

"Then it's good-by?" Pat asked.

"For a little while."

Peter's eyes twinkled.

"I'll be coming along myself on Christmas Eve."

Pat protested. "Oh, no. You must be mistaken!"

"I am not mistaken. I am like my creatures—I know when my time has come."

He shook Pat's hand.

"I wonder," he said, with awkward shyness, "if you'd do something for me."

"Anything I can, of course."

"Would you be willing to speak to God in my behalf?"

Pat was taken by surprise. He stammered: "I'm afraid I'm not worthy—"

"The message is urgent," Peter insisted.

"Then it might be quicker to pray," Pat said. "I've heard that prayer is like a rocket—powerful and fast!"

"But you will stand before the throne itself," Peter interrupted. "Today."

Pat met the old man's eyes. "Very well," he said finally. "What is it you want me to say?"

Peter hesitated. When he spoke, it was with a certain reluctance. He explained that he had made very little money over the summer. It had been his custom, for many years, to peddle his carvings in town. . . . But he had found the long hike too strenuous . . . and few tourists had found their way to his house.

Now, with the great storms of winter at hand, there was no feed stored away in his sheds. No feed for his creatures—the dogs and cats, the goats, the deer, the small red foxes, the rabbits and birds and skunks and raccoons and bear. . . .

"It will snow as never before, this winter," he went on. "And on Christmas Eve, I myself must climb the mountain. Tell Him this: tell Him my creatures will come to me for food, and I will be gone—the sheds will be empty. . . . He will understand. He will send someone to take my place. I have no doubt. No doubt at all!"

After a moment Pat said: "We'll deliver your message, of course."

He glanced quickly at Alicia.

To his immense relief, she said: "That's a promise!" There was no trace of mockery in her voice.

The old man stood for a moment in silence, his face working with emotion, his eyes blurred with difficult tears. Then he said: "Thank you. Thank you both." And, speaking to the dogs, he turned

41 ✦✿✦✿

abruptly away. It seemed to Pat that his step lagged, and he hurried after him.

"Take my staff, sir," he urged. The "sir" was instinctive; Pat had been trained to recognize moral strength in men.

"I will prepare my own staff," Peter said, smiling, "in good time."

Pat stopped as if he had heard a command. He said awkwardly:

"We'll be seeing you! Christmas Eve!"

"And that's a promise, too!" Peter called back.

He lifted his hand in farewell and went on, down the trail. They watched him until he disappeared into the shadows of the forest.

19

"What a wonderful old man!" Alicia whispered. "We ought to be ashamed of ourselves. We lied to him, through our teeth!"

"Did we?"

"Oh, Pat!" she laughed, but there was a note of reproof in her laughter. "You didn't really fall for that nonsense!"

"You did."

"Maybe for a minute—he was so sure! But we're moderns, remember? Straight thinkers. . . . What came over us?"

Pat met her eyes; he was aware of the healing silence of this high place—an enveloping peace and stillness.

"I don't know about you," he said, "but I'm going on to the top of the mountain."

"*Now* who thinks we're dead?"

"I do."

"We couldn't be! I feel so alive! It's a crazy idea! Death isn't like this. People just *stop*, don't they?"

"Let's go on, together," Pat said, "and find out."

"No! I'm afraid to! We might never come back!"

"And what's wrong with that?"

"What's *wrong* with it?"

Alicia stared at Pat, amazed.

"Why, Pat Adams, don't you like being alive? *I* do! I can think of a thousand reasons why!"

"For instance?"

"Oh—music and coffee and hot baths and hats and spring and flying—"

She caught her breath.

"And you."

43

"On the level?"

She nodded and went to him. He caught her close and they kissed. The kiss lasted a long time . . . it was deep and tender and grateful.

"We can prove we're alive," she whispered after a while. "If people can see us, then we're alive! And if we are alive, we can start all over again!"

Her body felt warm and real in his arms.

"We'll never forget this experience, Pat. Maybe it had to happen—to put us straight with ourselves."

Pat lifted his head and looked up at the mountain. He thought: "If I were alone, I'd keep my promise to Peter. I'd go on. . . ." But Alicia wanted life. Her arms were strong, her lips sweet. And so he said: "Okay. We'll go down and see!"

Hand in hand then they started back through the forest, making a wide detour to avoid the stone house in the clearing.

20

It was nine o'clock when they approached the Snow Creek bridge and saw that a string of cars had parked near the break in the railing. A crowd of accident-minded motorists stared at the crumpled car on the floor of the canyon.

Alicia stopped. "I feel foolish carrying this staff," she protested. "What'll I do with it, Pat?"

"Give it to me."

He hid both staffs beside the road, marking the spot with a pyramid of small stones. As they went forward again, he had an almost unendurable sensation of suspense, of profound anxiety.

A motor cop detached himself from the crowd and hurried along the bridge, yelling: "Hey! *You!*"

"He sees us," Alicia whispered. Her eyes were suddenly brilliant with relief. *"Oh, Pat! He sees us!"*

The cop shouted again!

"Is that your car down there?"

"It was," Pat admitted, trying to keep it light.

"Where in hell have you been?"

Pat explained.

"Pete Fauner, eh? Fooled him, didn't you?"

"What do you mean?"

"Oh, the old man's a little off," the cop said cheerfully. "He claims he can see the ghosts of people killed on the bridge. When you turned up last night, I'll bet he thought—"

The cop broke off and stared at Pat and Alicia with sudden sharp interest.

"You sure were lucky to come out of that wreck alive!"

The crowd stood back from the broken railing. Their expressions were puzzled, a little disappointed, as if they had expected, perhaps hoped for, a bloody finale.

Pat felt sick at his stomach when he looked down at the convertible.

"Where's your driver's license?"

The cop squinted at the card.

"Adams, Patrick," he read aloud.

"And I'm Adams, Alicia!"

She said it as if she expected, and wanted, a reaction. She got it. The officer looked up with a flash of interest in the settled skepticism of his eyes. "You're the singer?"

"That's me."

"Say! I've heard you on the radio! You sure have a swell voice!"

Alicia thanked him sweetly. She drew herself up a little and touched her hair and smiled her professional smile, her radio-star smile. *"Here we go again,"* Pat thought with a sudden sinking of the heart. He saw what she was after and turned away to conceal the expression he knew must be in his eyes.

The motor cop wrote down the vital statistics, but he was busy appraising Alicia's charms. He added her up, got the inevitable total, and, because she asked him to, flagged a Greyhound that charged down the grade bound for San Francisco.

"This lady's in a hurry," he shouted at the driver. "Step on it, Mac!"

21

The crowded bus fled toward Alicia's deadline. Pat sat beside a fat man with a lap full of Christmas packages. Alicia was across the aisle, squeezed in between two young sailors who watched her with rotating jaws, their heads turned stiffly at an identical angle.

Speed and roar . . . the terrible urgency of oversize tires on asphalt. . . . The dream receding . . . the house . . . the clock . . . the forest . . . erased by the onrushing reality of signboards, gas stations, oil derricks, hamburger stands, boulevard stops. . . .

The first fifty miles were a nightmare of speed and confusion, and Pat, who was never comfortable unless he himself was at the wheel, spent a tense hour. The bus bored westward at an implacable sixty, then, with a screech of brakes, swerved and stopped.

"Half an hour for lunch, folks!"

Alicia was frantic. She stared into a cup of coffee while Pat tried to get the radio station on the phone. Before he could complete the call, the passengers began piling into the bus again and he had to sprint for it.

22

The sailors had disappeared. Pat moved across and sat beside Alicia. He wondered whether she remembered last night. She had pressed against him in her sleep, curving to his need of her. But now, impatient and nervous, she cried out: "Why can't he drive *faster*? I'll never make it!"

"Do you care?"

"Of course I do!"

"I thought we were going to start all over again!"

"I never said I'd give up my job! I love it, Pat! You know I do!"

"Okay. But we're going on together, aren't we? No divorce?"

As if to avoid an answer, she put her hand on his wrist, but it was only to push back his sleeve so that she could look at his watch.

"No divorce?" Pat insisted.

She opened a newspaper one of the sailors had left and turned to the radio log. As if nothing else mattered, she studied the broadcast schedules, humming under her breath.

Pat let the question ride until they reached the city.

Then, in a speeding taxi, fighting time and traffic with nerves like taut steel wires, he asked her again:

"I've got to know, Alicia. Now. Did you mean what you said this morning?"

They were edging into the curb in front of the radio station. Alicia's hand was on the door. She jumped out before the taxi stopped, dodged through the crowd on the sidewalk, and disappeared into the building.

Pat paid the driver and followed her. She had disappeared into the studio from which, in exactly one minute, her program was scheduled to go on the air.

The announcer's voice came over the loudspeaker as Pat opened the door. Alicia's accompanist sat at the piano, waiting nervously to fill in if it was necessary.

Alicia gasped: *"I made it! I'm here!"* and ran to her mike, shedding the torn coat and with a defiant gesture shaking back her hair. . . .

Pat grabbed her arms and held her.

"You'll tell me now."

Her eyes blazed at him.

"We're on the air, you fool!"

"To hell with that. Answer me. Do you want a divorce?"

"Yes. *Yes.* I do!"

He let her go.

The suave baritone of the announcer gave Alicia to her public:

"The songs you love to hear, sung by the girl you love to love. *Ladies and gentlemen—Alicia Adams!"*

23

Pat walked home.

The flat was cold and in disorder. A pair of Alicia's bedroom slippers stood pigeon-toed in the middle of their room. Her negligée lay across a chair.

Pat switched on the radio and dialed until he found her. *"My darling, my darling,"* she sang. That mellow, loving voice of hers! Not great. Not important. Except to him.

He went back to the sitting-room and stood at the window, looking at the city. The sun still burnished the tops of the buildings, but the streets were in shadow. The Christmas crowd poured from the shops, laden with packages, and fought for transportation on windy corners.

It was after dark when, at last, Alicia phoned:

"Pat, I'm not coming home. I've taken a room at the St. Francis. What happened this morning was just our imagination. We were crazy to believe any of it."

"Were we?"

"This is reality, Pat. Not that. . . . We can't just live for love."

"Can't we?"

"Oh, Pat, stop asking foolish questions! Send my things over, will you? It's easier if we don't have to see each other again."

"Okay."

There was a silence; it lasted so long that Pat thought she had hung up. Then he heard her voice, blurred and strange:

"Pat. It was wonderful being married to you. . . . But I guess war spoiled me for a wife. I like excitement and adventure and risk. . . ."

"Call me," he managed to say. "Any time."

He hung up, fumbling for the hook, unsteady, not trusting his voice. At first he felt only amazement that she could stab him so expertly through the heart. . . . She liked risk! How about bearing children?

He packed her things.

At the last minute, before closing the suitcases, he hesitated before a photograph of himself in uniform. Alicia liked it because the ribbons were on the wrong side. He had pinned them there when the jacket was on a hanger, and the switch had always made Alicia laugh.

He decided against sending it to her. Instead he tore the picture across and threw the pieces out of the window. The cold wind snatched and scattered them. . . .

He took the suitcases to the St. Francis, and, unable to face a night alone in the flat, checked in at a downtown hotel.

In the morning he quit his job. Then, in fact, he was alone.

24

The city had never been a happier place. Yet Pat had no feeling for holly and tinsel.

His mother expected him to bring Alicia for dinner on Christmas Day. He couldn't tell her, with the holiday spirit making everybody nostalgic and tender, that Alicia had left him. On the phone he invented an excuse so obviously false that his mother hung up in the middle of it. He called her back. She mustn't think, he protested, that he didn't want to be with her.

"Very well, dear," his mother interrupted. "Don't try to explain. I *understand*. And, dear? *Merry Christmas!*"

He sent her perfume, and a package of books went to his father. He said nothing to them about the accident, nor did he confide in them his curious feeling that every day, from here on, would be his only if he met the payments; he was in debt—not to a bank, either.

He hesitated to send Alicia a gift, but finally three gold bracelets went to her by messenger. Pat's card, with the Adams scratched out, and "Love" scrawled across the back, was enclosed. But no address. No phone number. . . . He reckoned that this might fetch her.

And it did.

He returned to his hotel to find a message: "Call Miss Adams."

Miss Adams!

He went to his room and sat on the bed in the dark, trying to understand himself. The truth was: he was lonely. Without Alicia he was always lonely, even in a crowd.

He smoked half a pack of cigarettes before he called her.

"Pat? Is that you, at last? I've been trying to get you all day. Fred told me where you were."

"Fred?"

"The bartender at the Rio. I called *him*, finally.
. . . I've something to tell you. They want me in
New York. Television. They say I have the looks
for it. And the voice. . . . Are you listening?"

"Of course."

"I'm flying east day after tomorrow."

She faltered; then, lightly:

"Now tell me about you! Any plans?"

"No plans."

"I wish I could talk to you."

"Why not?"

"Tomorrow? After my broadcast?"

"Where?"

"Wait for me at the Rio."

25

He slept very little that night, still unable to shake
off the conviction that this was some sort of re-
prieve, that he was on probation. He thought:
"Work's the answer. I guess it's up to me to stop
talking about that book and *write* it."

His mind went back to Snow Creek, the stone
house in the forest.

If he could spend a year up there. . . . He had no desire to retreat from perilous times, from challenging problems. But he must write about a single day at Hatten, while he still remembered. Not an uncensored record of battle. A look, rather, at the mental carnage. This Pat had known, and still knew, and could perhaps put into words. A grain of sand in a mountain of evidence? Yes. But important, if it were added, or if it were taken away. . . .

In the morning he walked uptown, trying to kill time. The wind tasted of ice; people leaned against it with their heads down. Word had come of a blizzard in the Sierras and Pat wondered how Peter was making out in that ragged sweater of his, the thin-soled shoes. . . . Suddenly, Pat recalled having promised to deliver a message. . . .

He stopped short.

The gusty, bitter wind carried snatches of recorded carols along the streets of the city. Sleigh bells jingled when the doors of toyshops opened. Coins rang in Salvation Army pots. . . .

"I suppose I could pray," Pat thought, fumbling in his mind for extenuation. He was not familiar with ritual, had never knelt before an altar.

He went on, looking vaguely for a church. But

when he found one, he turned away, embarrassed and desolate, not daring to enter.

He decided that he needed a drink, a stiff one, to blur the outlines. . . .

26

The Rio was empty.

With a nod to Fred, Pat climbed on a stool and ordered a hooker of rum. The first drink only increased the too inclusive range of his consciousness; it took three to establish an endurable norm.

"Where's the missus?" Fred wanted to know. "Ain't she coming in today?"

"Later."

Then things got clear again. Too clear. It seemed important to make Fred understand.

"Do you believe in anything, Fred?"

"Sure. I believe in lots of things."

"Now, get this. There's a mountain."

"Yeah?"

"You can't see it, can you?"

"No."

"But if I can make you *believe* it's there—it *is!*"

"It is?"

"You don't get it."

"Get what?"

"I'm talking about faith." Pat stared darkly into his drink. "Faith," he repeated. "It's coming up for a test pretty soon."

"How's that?"

"The scientists are working on it. Final test of faith. . . . Better watch out, Fred. Better have faith. Or else!"

"After three rums," Fred wailed, "always they talk about the atom bomb! Have another. Fog you up again."

"Thanks, fella! You'll pray for me, won't you?"

"Me?" The bartender's expression of morose boredom broke into what, for him, must have been a grin. "Me, pray?"

"How's it done, Fred?"

Fred spun a glass of rum across the counter into Pat's hand. "You can't fake it. That's all I know."

Several people came into the bar, drank, and departed. Softly a wall radio murmured to itself. But the television screen was blank.

At four o'clock Alicia came on the air:

"*My darling . . . my darling . . . my darling. . . .*"

"There's the missus," Fred said. "You're a lucky fella. You got a girl like that, and you think about religion!"

27

Just before five a noisy crowd filled the place; Pat was hemmed in by laughing girls and their men. But he kept an eye on the entrance, watching for Alicia, her brilliant presence, her lustrous beauty, so clean and shining. She didn't come. And when Fred handed him the phone, he knew he hadn't expected her to come.

She sounded far away and nervous. She couldn't make it. . . . And something about vice-presidents—the stock radio joke. . . . "You know tomorrow's Christmas Eve—my last day!"

"Christmas Eve," Pat repeated. "Old Peter Fauner's last day, too."

"Must we talk about that now?"

"We made a promise. Remember?"

Trying to head him off, she said: "I *love* the bracelets! What do *you* want for Christmas?"

The answer was there, unequivocal, simple. *Not to be alone.* . . . But he said nothing.

"I'll send the John Dewey books from New York," she said.

And then, with a trace of panic in her voice:

"*Pat!* You've been drinking, haven't you?"

"Yes," he said. "But I'm remembering the fire-light and the forest."

"And *I'm* remembering the world we live in! Good-by, Pat. Merry Christmas!"

He fumbled with the receiver and Fred took the instrument.

"What's the matter? She stood you up?"

Pat shouldered his way through the crowd and went out into the street. It was dark and there was no wind; the air seemed frozen. He signaled a taxi, gave the driver the name of his hotel, took a deep breath, and blacked out.

28

Someone must have piloted him to his room. When he woke, he was lying on the bed. His over-coat had been folded neatly over the back of a chair; his hat was on the dresser. Whoever it was— a porter, probably—had covered him with a blanket. "This calls for a five-dollar tip," Pat thought gratefully. He sat up and swung his legs over the side of the bed. He felt all right. Nine o'clock!

He got to his feet, testing his equilibrium, and wavered to the window. Outside, the light was strange, and, pressing his forehead against the cold comfort of the glass, he saw that it was snowing.

Thick and soft and silent the snow fell like gauze over the city. Roofs and sills were white. Cars in the street below wore ermine. And Pat could hear a shovel ringing on asphalt where someone was clearing a path across the sidewalk.

He took a shower, dressed, and went downstairs to the coffee-room for breakfast. The newspapers headlined the weather: "Sixty-Mile Gales in Mother Lode Country . . . Sierras Facing Record Snowfall . . . Cars Stalled . . . Trains Halted by Drifts. . . ."

And once more, as three-dimensional as if he were looking into a stereopticon, Peter Fauner's stone house appeared in Pat's mind.

"Suppose he hasn't cut enough wood for that fireplace of his. . . . Suppose he runs out of food! I'd better get to him while I still can!"

Pat decided as quickly as that: the plan was made

before he'd gulped down his first cup of coffee.

On a chance, he called Alicia. Something he'd said the night before might have reached her heart. Might have set in motion certain dormant memories, reminding her of the dream, the promise, and the hope. . . .

But the operator at the St. Francis said: "Sorry. Miss Adams's room doesn't answer."

So. That was that.

Pat hung up with a vicious slam of the receiver into the cradle. Grabbing his heaviest coat and a couple of sweaters, he sought a drive-yourself car service and rented a station wagon.

"I'll need chains. And I'm in a hurry!"

He shopped at one of the big mail-order houses on Market Street, where it was possible to buy everything under one roof: a leather windbreaker for Peter . . . boots . . . socks . . . flannel shirts . . . a long, knitted muffler. . . . Then bacon, flour, eggs, butter, coffee—straight down the list—biscuits for the dogs, canned fish for the cats, bird seed. . . . And, from a feed store on the edge of town, two bales of hay and a sack of oats!

He felt better, somehow, when the purchases were safely packed into the car.

He left the city at noon, drove away from the

merriment, the good cheer, the fine, hearty ringing of bells, into the silent, frozen country.

The snow turned into sleet; the roads were glassy, the shoulders hard as flint. Pat's arms ached from wrestling with the wheel. But hour after hour, even after he was too tired to drive another mile, he kept on.

As he crossed the valley, the sky grew darker and heavier. Late in the afternoon it began to snow again, only now it was not sugary city snow; these flakes were thick as wool. They fell straight, soundlessly, smothering the earth.

Pat drew off the road and put on the chains. . . . He was hungry and cold. He slapped his hands together and stamped and got into the car again. He faced now the long, final upgrade—about fifty miles.

It was past eight o'clock when at last he saw the Snow Creek bridge. The long span looked as airy and as fragile as a web—a thing of delicate, immaterial beauty. Below, the forest was weighted with snow, the trees motionless, the creek silent, too, beneath a surface coating of ice. . . . There must have been a moon behind the clouds, because a clear radiance, like crystal, illumined the fantastic scene.

Pat drove across and found a shallow parking space at the foot of the pass. He locked the car and stood at the top of the path near the buttress, looking for Peter Fauner's light. His heart pounded. This was a lofty place, and he was dog-tired, but he was excited, too. He realized now that during all those hours of fast driving there had been in the back of his mind, unacknowledged, the fear that he might find Peter gone. . . .

Then, with a pang of relief, he saw the light. It shook once, a golden star in the whiteness, then vanished. . . .

29

As Pat approached the clearing, he saw that the deer were there. They stood in a semicircle, heads lifted, motionless even when he moved toward them. All around the house and on the roof the creatures waited. And the snow fell on them softly, veil after veil. . . .

Pat shouted: "Peter!"

He pounded on the door. Inside, the dogs set up a frantic barking.

"Peter!"

There was no answer. Pat hoisted himself up and tried to see through the window, but from that angle, and with so deep an embrasure, nothing was visible except a far corner of the room.

Finally he forced the door. He had to.

The dogs rushed at him, then retreated, step by step, bristling along their spines, until they stood beside the old man's chair.

Peter Fauner sat before the fire; the moving light flickered over him. His hands were folded. His eyes were closed. Before him, leaning against the stone of the fireplace, the staff. . . .

Pat stood for a moment on the threshold. He said softly: "Peter! Are you asleep?" The warmth of the room flowed around him. He heard the ticking and tocking of the clock, and was swept suddenly by a sense of dignity and mastery and exultation. Peter was gone. The sentience no one can explain was no longer in the body that sat there.

Pat spoke reassuringly to the dogs. Leaving the door open, he went to Peter and touched the cold hands.

Then, remembering the staff, he turned to examine it. The name *Peter Fauner* had been recently carved in the wood. . . . Why, if Peter had climbed the mountain, hadn't he taken his staff with him?

A kind of spiritual gall, poisonous and bitter, flooded Pat's heart. He might have known—it had been his imagination, all of it. Fairy-book stuff. Fantasy. Alicia was right—best to stick by reality, the unequivocal fact, the testimony of the senses!

He put the staff back against the fireplace and went toward the open door. On the threshold he paused. A darting disk of light flashed in the trees across the clearing. For a second, fear of the supernatural made his scalp crawl. Then he heard Alicia's voice:

"Pat? Is that you?"

He ran down to the gate.

"Alicia!" he shouted. "Alicia!"

She struggled toward him through the deep drifts, her head and shoulders powdered with snow.

"*Pat*—I thought you'd be here! I had to come, too! I couldn't stop thinking of him. Is he all right?"

"He's dead, Alicia."

"Oh, *Pat!*"

"You aren't afraid to go in?"

"No. No. I want to."

They stood beside the chair.

Alicia whispered: "He *did* know, didn't he?— that he'd go on Christmas Eve?"

She looked up, her eyes shimmering with tears. "You'll think I'm silly, Pat—but this morning I went to church, and prayed. I haven't for years. I wasn't too good at it. But I said what we promised to say, remember? *Please send someone to care for Peter Fauner's creatures.*"

Suddenly she caught her breath.

"Pat! *We've* been sent! Don't you see? I *did* get through! I *was* heard! We're *here!*"

"That's right," Pat said slowly. Again he felt the exquisite fire of belief in his veins. "I'm going to stay here all winter, if I can."

"Me too."

Alicia put her arms around him.

"I decided this morning. I'm giving you myself. My Christmas present, darling! With all the good wishes in the world. And my love."

She smiled. "We got our second chance, didn't we? To be together? To make it work?"

"This time it will," Pat said.

He braced himself. He'd have to tell her, now, about Peter's staff. . . .

She listened, then shook her head. Her eyes were suddenly clear and brilliant with happiness.

"That doesn't throw me," she said. "How much proof do we *need*, anyway? Isn't it enough to know that if you pray, you'll be heard?"

Together, then, they struggled through the snow back to the bridge. Alicia had rented a car and a driver, who waited, parked behind the station wagon.

Pat explained what had happened, and instructed the man to go on to the nearest town and make a report.

"Okay, sir. It may take a couple of hours."

"We'll wait. Tell the police Peter Fauner's place. They'll know where to find us."

Pat and Alicia went back to the house in the forest.

When Pat opened the door, he saw that Peter's body was still there before the fire. But the staff had disappeared.

A NOTE ON THE TYPE

This book is set in Monotype BELL, *a copy of the English Monotype face of the same name. The Englishman* JOHN BELL *(1745–1831) was responsible for the original cutting of this design. The vocations of Bell were many—among a few might be mentioned bookseller, printer, publisher, typefounder, and journalist. His types were considerably influenced by the delicacy and beauty of the French copperplate engravers. Monotype Bell might also be classified as a delicate and refined rendering of Scotch Roman.*

Composed, printed, and bound by KINGSPORT PRESS, INC., *Kingsport, Tennessee. Typography and binding design by* GEORGE SALTER.